BRIDGET & BOT

Written & Illustrated by
Sequoia Bostick

KAEDEN ♥ BOOKS™

Title: Bridget and Bot
Copyright © 2017 Kaeden Corporation
Author: Sequoia Bostick
Illustrator: Sequoia Bostick

ISBN: 978-1-61181-519-1 (paperback)

Published by:
    Kaeden Corporation
    P. O. Box 16190
    Rocky River, Ohio 44116
    1-(800)-890-READ(7323)
    www.kaeden.com

Printed in Guangzhou, China
NOR/0117/CA21602022

First edition 2017

Bridget, the young inventor, has a problem. She ABSOLUTELY, POSITIVELY, has nothing to do. Earlier that morning her papa packed up his tools for the Inventors Convention. No children were allowed to go. Bridget had to stay behind and watch the workshop.

"It's not so bad, I'm sure you will find something to do. Just stay out of trouble while I'm away." said Papa.

"Papa's right," thought Bridget. "As an inventor, I have to invent my own fun." She had to do something, but what? She went to the workshop to think.

She thought . . .

and thought . . .

and thought until
finally . . .

"I'VE
GOT IT!!!"

Bridget would build a friend and together they would play. That way she'd always have someone to keep her company when her father left on a trip.

8

She got out her paper and
whipped out a quick sketch.
She got to work without
any delay.

9

CLANK

CLANK

TONK

Her invention was completed in no time. She took a step back to look at her new robot.

"I think I will call him Bot for now," said Bridget.

"Now that the work is done, it is time to have some fun."

With a couple of winds of his key and a clonk to his head, Bot was up, running, and ready to GO!

Bridget and Bot had the entire workshop to themselves.

"LETS PLAY!" shouted Bridget.
Bot buzzed and followed.

They raced jet
packs through
the house,

and made a mess in
the kitchen.

They pretended to venture
out and discover strange
new creatures.

18

They played . . .

and played . . .

and played . . .

and played . . . until the sun
began to set. Bridget was tired
and decided to settle down.

21

"It's time for bed," said Bridget to Bot. Bot was not tired. Bot was a robot and did not need sleep. Bot had a glitch. He continued to play and play.

He jumped on the bed
until it broke.

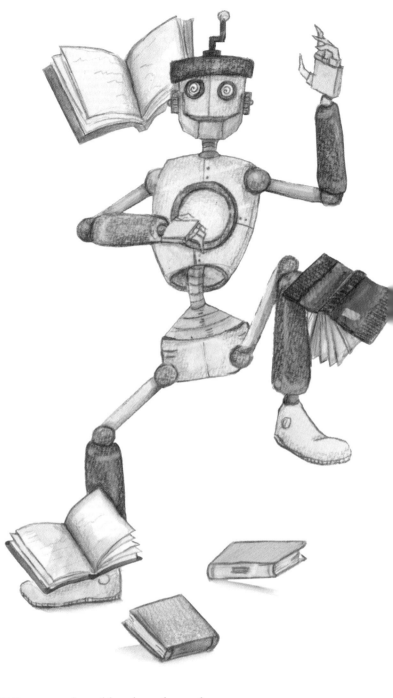

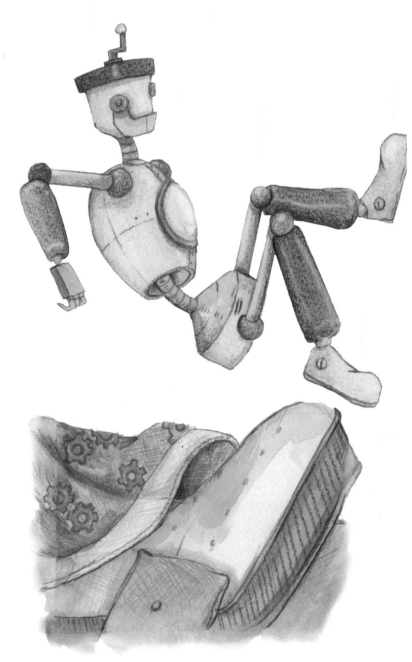

He took all the books
off the shelf.

Bridget tried to stop him but he
was too fast. Bot played . . .

and played . . .

and played.

Finally Bridget
screamed,

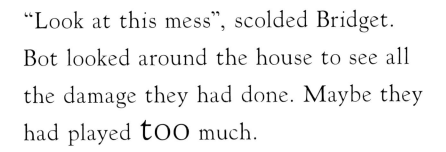

"Look at this mess", scolded Bridget.
Bot looked around the house to see all
the damage they had done. Maybe they
had played too much.

"We have to clean up this house before
Papa gets home," Bridget said.

They got to work right away.
They fixed the broken bed.
They put the books away.
They cleaned . . .

and cleaned . . .

and cleaned . . .

until finally the house
was spotless.

Bridget shut Bot down
and put him away.

Just as she finished cleaning up her papa returned. "GOOD evening Papa!" Bridget shouted, surprising her father at the door.

"Hello Bridget, how was your day?" asked her Papa.

33

"It was great, Papa!
I made a new friend and
I cannot wait to show
him to you."

34